LIZARD
meets
Ivana the Terrible

LIZARD
meets
Ivana the Terrible

C. Anne Scott

Illustrated by
Stephanie Roth

A
LITTLE
APPLE
PAPERBACK

SCHOLASTIC INC.

New York Toronto London Auckland Sydney
Mexico City New Delhi Hong Kong Buenos Aires

ISBN 0-439-21999-X

Published by Scholastic Inc., 555 Broadway, New York, NY 10012,
by arrangement with Henry Holt and Company, LLC.
SCHOLASTIC, LITTLE APPLE, and associated logos are trademarks
and/or registered trademarks of Scholastic Inc.

12 11 10 9 8 7 6 5 4 3   2 3 4 5 6/0

Printed in the U.S.A.   40

First Scholastic printing, October 2001

LIZARD
meets
Ivana the Terrible

Chapter 1

"Don't like Erma Malone. She never takes a bath."

"Don't like Brady Brootski. He's a big brat."

"You can like us."

It was Lizzie Gardener's first day of third grade at Morningside Elementary, and she didn't know anyone. Feeling as helpless as a mouse, she wanted to disappear into the classroom locker beside her. *I'd rather be in a mush pot,* she thought.

The gossipy girls rattled out their names—"Tiffy" and "Crystal." It was hard for Lizzie to remember who was who. With long brown hair tied up in feathery bows and fluttery dresses splashed with bright oranges, greens, and yellows,

they resembled talking parrots. Tiffy talked the
most. Crystal copied her. They talked alike and
almost looked alike, except Crystal had a patch of
freckles across her nose, and she popped and
chomped her bubble gum.

"Oh, no. Here comes Ivana!" said Tiffy as a girl
with crazy hair came their way. Lizzie couldn't

help but stare at her from top to toe. Her long black hair shot out in so many directions, it looked like a fireworks display. She was dressed funny, too, in striped overalls like a railroad conductor. Her muddy hiking boots made a loud stomping noise.

"And you definitely don't want to like her," said Tiffy, loud enough for the girl to hear.

"No way," added Crystal.

As Ivana passed by, she shot Tiffy and Crystal a glare that could freeze fire. "Hssss," she said between her teeth as she balled up her fist at them.

Lizzie was shocked. "Who—who's that?" she stammered.

Tiffy and Crystal leaned closer. "Ivana the Terrible," they echoed each other.

"She can turn you to stone with one stare," whispered Tiffy.

"Yeah. One look and you're a rock," repeated Crystal.

"She has snakes growing out of her hair," Tiffy said, wriggling her fingers all over her head.

"She's so scary" —Crystal leaned so close, she fogged Lizzie's glasses with her breath— "she even cracked the mirror in the girls' bathroom when she looked into it."

"Swear," they both said at once, crossing their fingers. Their voices darted at Lizzie like the tongues of dragons.

Suddenly a boy two heads taller than anyone broke into their circle and towered over Lizzie. As she looked up at him, he twisted the gold stud in his left earlobe. On his ragged, stained T-shirt was a picture of a killer frog wearing a spiked collar.

"So, you're the new girl," he said. "What's your name?"

"Lizzie," she squeaked.

Brady grinned.

"No one's talking to you, Brady Brootski," snapped Tiffy, "so talk to the hand." She flashed the palm of her hand in his face.

"Yeah," said Crystal, popping her gum, "talk to the hand."

Brady looked into Tiffy's hand like it was a mirror and smoothed his hand through his hair. "Lizzie, huh? That's a stupid name. Sounds like Lizard."

Brady cackled a hyena laugh and walked away as the bell rang. Lizzie's eyes followed him. His greasy blond hair was short except for a long, thin braid that fell down his back like a rope. On the back of his T-shirt blazed the words *Beware of Frog.*

"Class, please take your seats," called their teacher, Mrs. Lula. She motioned for Lizzie to stand beside her. Mrs. Lula asked Lizzie for the *All About Me* card she was supposed to fill out.

"I want to introduce our new student," she said, looking first at Lizzie and then at her card. Lizzie hung her head, then raised it just enough

to peek around the room. She saw Tiffy waving at her from the third row. Crystal pointed at a girl in the front row.

"That's Erma," she mouthed, and held her nose.

The classroom was full. Lizzie saw only one empty chair. It sat behind *Hissing Girl with Crazy Hair* and in front of *Beware of Frog Boy*. Lizzie closed her eyes, gulped, and inched closer to her teacher.

"This is Lizzie Gardener," began Mrs. Lula. So far, she was the only person Lizzie was sure she liked. Mrs. Lula smelled like honeysuckle and wore a dress with big red polka dots. Her voice flitted around the room as gentle as butterfly wings.

Lizzie worried, in fact, that Mrs. Lula might be the only friend she ever made in this strange place. In her old school, she was too shy to make a best friend. Lizzie hoped she could make one here.

For a second, Lizzie dared to look up. Something on the back wall caught her eye: a giant mural of a life-size cheetah, dotted with only a few spots. Above the cheetah, painted in big, black letters, was *World's Fastest Readers*. The cheetah looked so lifelike, Lizzie imagined it might run off the wall. Her eyes swept back to her classmates, who stared at her, unblinking.

"Lizzie comes to Texas from Florida, the Sunshine State," Mrs. Lula continued. "Now, this is exciting. Right now, her father is cruising the North Atlantic in a Coast Guard cutter. While he's on duty overseas, Lizzie has come to live with her grandmother. And my goodness, it says here your grandmother is a clown."

Lizzie's ears vibrated with her classmates' whispers. *I wish I'd left off the clown part*, she thought.

"So, Lizzie, what do you like to do?" asked Mrs. Lula.

Lizzie's throat pipes choked shut. She dropped her head and stared at the toes of her penny loafers. They were her favorite pair of shoes. Her grandma Lil had polished them as bright as the new copper pennies in her shoes. Lizzie wished she could take the penny out of each shoe and cover her eyes with them so she couldn't see the class staring at her.

She could feel everything slipping down, the

red scrunchie sliding down her long blond pony-tail, her glasses slipping down her nose, and even her kneesocks. Lizzie quickly leaned over to pull up her socks and her glasses fell to the floor. Everyone started snickering. Brady cackled the loudest. Mrs. Lula turned a stern look on the class.

"Now, everyone, please tell Lizzie hello."

"Hello, Lizzie," said the class.

"Hello, Lizard," said Brady Brootski.

Mrs. Lula didn't hear him say it, but Lizzie did. So did Ivana the Terrible. She twisted in her seat and pointed at him, holding out her arm like a sword. "You're the lizard, Brady. Even your mama says so!" she shouted.

That's it. I'm out of here, thought Lizzie, but she couldn't move. Her feet were blocks of cement.

"Ivana!" scolded Mrs. Lula. She held up a long piece of blue chalk. Ivana stomped to the front, took the chalk, and proceeded to the board. She wrote her name in all capital letters. She slammed the chalk down on the tray so hard, the chalk broke in two. Then she stomped back to her desk.

"Let me show you to your assigned seat," said Mrs. Lula. She shepherded Lizzie like a lost lamb to *the desk.* When she passed Ivana, she didn't dare look her in the eye. She feared she'd be turned to stone.

As she eased into her seat, Brady Brootski bumped her chair from behind. In Lizzie's imagination she heard a terrible snapping noise. It was the sound of a giant mousetrap clamping shut on its victim.

Ding, ding, ding. "Good morning, girls and boys." The voice on the intercom belonged to Mrs. Hog, the principal. "Welcome back from spring break. I hope everyone had a fun time. Now clap if you are glad the State Test of Achievement in Reading—the STAR test," she said in a dramatic tone, "is *over.*"

The class broke out in hoots and whistles and very few claps. Brady drummed on his desk.

"I still want you to keep on reading, though, so I'm making a promise to you this morning. Is everyone listening carefully?"

The room settled into a deep, rare silence.

"If even one class manages to earn more than a thousand points in Supersonic Reader before the awards assembly, then I, Mrs. Hog, will kiss a hog."

The students began to wiggle and giggle in their seats. Lizzie wondered what Supersonic Reader was. Did it have anything to do with the cheetah on the wall?

"Wait. There's more. Are you listening?" The microphone screeched loud enough to make Lizzie howl. Hands flew to ears and back down again in time to hear ". . . principal for a day!"

"What did she say? Are we getting a new principal today?" The class peppered Mrs. Lula with questions.

She responded, "Mrs. Hog said that the student who earns the most Supersonic Reader points by the awards assembly will get to be principal for a day. Ivana, if you keep flying through those books, I'd say that principal might be you. Right now you lead, with fifteen points!"

Erma Malone and Mrs. Lula were the only ones who clapped. Everyone else rolled their eyes, and some kids began whispering to one another. Tiffy flashed her "talk to the hand" at Ivana, and Crystal copied her. Ivana stood up anyway, took a bow, and clapped back at Erma and Mrs. Lula. They all three shared a smile.

"Ivana, you may dot the cheetah's spots this morning," said Mrs. Lula, and handed Ivana a stamp. Each student took a turn calling out the Supersonic Reader points they had earned since the last spotting. Ivana stamped a dot on the cheetah for every point.

After she had stamped on the last spot, everyone followed the direction to pull out their spiral notebooks and begin writing. Lizzie didn't know what to do. Mrs. Lula stopped by her desk. A honeysuckle smell swirled all around. "Lizzie," she said, "right now we're writing in our buddy journals. Every morning you write a letter to your assigned buddy. Then you swap journals and read each other's letter. Ivana will be your buddy."

Chapter 2

March 23

Dear Ivana,

Hi. How are you? I am fine. My name
is Lizzie Gardener. I am eight years old.
I really like my Peruvian guinea pigs,
Samson and Delilah. I think Delilah is
pregnant. I don't know for sure. It's hard
to tell with guinea pigs. Do you have any
pets?

Your buddy,
Lizzie

P.S. Thanks for sticking up for me. Is
Brady Brootski nothing but trouble?

March 23

Dear Lizzie,

I'm glad you're my journal buddy now. Mrs. Lula has been my buddy all year. What was it like living in the Sunshine State? I went to the beach once. My brothers told me not to touch a jellyfish. As soon as we got there, I saw something weird on the beach. It looked like a blue balloon. I picked it up. It stung me. It was a jellyfish. My mom rushed me back to the kitchen. The cook put vinegar and meat ~~tenvi~~ tendrizz on my hand. It felt better after a while. Have you ever picked up a jellyfish?

Your buddy,
Ivana

P.S. Do you have a best friend?

P.P.S. Your hair is really long. Have you ever cut it?

After fifteen minutes the timer beeped, and everyone traded journals.

When Lizzie and Ivana wrote back to each other, this is what they wrote:

Dear Ivana,

No. I never picked up a jellyfish. I stepped on one. OUCH! It stung me so bad, I had a blister the size of a balloon. I thought I was turning into a jellyfish. I have a bunch of seashells. I have never cut my hair. My dad won't let me. He says my mom wanted it to grow long. She died when I was three.

Your buddy,

Lizzie

P.S. I don't have a best friend. I think it would be nice to have one.

Dear Lizzie,

Boy, do I have pets. You can come over and meet them. My favorite is Buster.

I'll tell you more about him later. Supersonic Reader started before spring break. What you do is read a book on the list. You have a zillion choices. It tells you how many points each book is worth. After you read it, you take a book test on the computer in the library. If you pass, you get points. Brady always brags that he just watches the movie on the book to get points. You can use your points to buy a prize in the library.

Your buddy,
Ivana

P.S. *Thirteen Ways to Sink a Sub* is a funny book. You can read it really fast and get four points and four spots on the cheetah. I got all those spots because I read *Does Third Grade Last Forever? Scorpions, Don't Call Me Toad!* and *After Fifth Grade, the World!* Did you ever want to rule the world?

P.P.S. Yes. Bratski's always trouble—if you're a girl!

During silent reading, Lizzie checked out *Thirteen Ways to Sink a Sub*. It *was* funny. But Lizzie finished it in a snap and then grew bored, so she stared at the back of Ivana's head. Not even Samson and Delilah had that much hair. Theirs was silky smooth. Ivana's was wild, like lightning bolts. And there were a couple of leaves stuck in it. Lizzie wondered if she climbed trees before she came to school. She had to lean over to see around all that hair.

Lizzie drifted back to her book but was soon interrupted by soft, whispery noises behind her. Quietly she turned around. She saw Brady Brootski pointing at the words with his finger as he slowly mouthed them out loud. When he

caught her staring at him, he jerked his hand away and flushed red. Lizzie's eyes fell on the title before he covered it with his arms. *Babar's Little Circus Star*? She figured Brady would probably be reading *Slime Time* or *Stinker from Space*, not a picture book about an elephant.

"What are you gawking at, Lizard?"

Lizzie didn't have a chance to answer because Ivana the Terrible answered for her. "Not much, Broot Beasssst," she hissed. Lizzie ducked her head, quick to avoid Ivana's eyes. She had to escape. She thought of a way and raised her hand.

"Yes, Lizzie?" asked Mrs. Lula.

"May I use the rest room?" she asked.

Mrs. Lula handed her a giant wooden pass with the word *Potty* painted on it. Lizzie wanted to die. *How embarrassing,* she thought. *I'm a third grader, not a kindergartner. Now the whole school will know I need to use the bathroom.* As Lizzie carried the potty pass down the hall, she tried to cover the word *Potty* with her arms. But it was no use. The word was too big.

In the bathroom, when Lizzie went to wash her hands, she saw it. The crack. The fabled crack. The one Crystal said Ivana had put there when she looked into the mirror. Lizzie was fascinated. She stared at the crack. What must it be like to have the power to crack the bathroom mirror with a single look?

It was true. Ivana was scary to look at. Besides

her black hair, wild as a jungle beast's, she had several teeth missing. *Too many trips from the tooth fairy,* thought Lizzie. Ivana was as thin as the stick people Lizzie liked to draw. And she was much taller than Lizzie. Everyone was. The only thing about Ivana that Lizzie couldn't describe was her eyes. She avoided those.

Lizzie stood on tiptoes to touch the top of the crack. She traced along it with her finger. It was like tracing the track of a dark teardrop sliding down a silver river. Lizzie felt a surge of power, like she was touching something magical. She wished she could feel that something magical about herself.

Yanking off her glasses, she fogged them with her breath and wiped them clean with a paper towel. Shoving on her glasses, she made a face at herself in the mirror and spoke to her reflection. "Who would want to be best friends with such a little mouse? A very shy mouse with glasses."

At lunchtime Tiffy and Crystal swept Lizzie off to their end of the lunch table. Tiffy and Crystal had matching pink lunch boxes with *Barbie* written in silver sparkly letters. Lizzie looked at her own lunch container—a cloth bag covered with pictures of pandas and the words *Save Endangered Wildlife*. She was the only one who had a reusable lunch sack. She hid it on her lap.

"So, Lizzie, what *do* you like to do?" asked Tiffy.

"Really. You never got to tell us this morning because of Bratski," said Crystal, chomping on her carrot stick.

Lizzie couldn't think of what to say. She liked to do lots of things, but there was one thing she loved the most.

"I like to read," she said, and bit into her bologna sandwich. Tomato juice ran down her arm.

"I bet you make straight A's," piped up Tiffy. "We could use a smart girl in our group. Will you help us with our homework sometimes?"

"Sure," said Lizzie. Actually, she felt unsure. She wondered if by *help*, Tiffy meant copying her homework.

"Well, I think books are boring," said Crystal.

Lizzie peeled back the top of her soggy bread. Grandma Lil had poked a huge tomato slice between the meat and cheese.

"Yuck. That looks nasty," Tiffy said, staring down at Lizzie's sandwich.

"It is," Lizzie replied.

"Here," offered Crystal, "I'll give you half of my pimento cheese."

"Thanks," said Lizzie, keeping her mouth busy by nibbling on the sandwich. She couldn't figure out what to say, so she said nothing. She listened to Tiffy talk about herself and soon grew restless. *I'll never make a real friend just listening,* she thought. Then her eye caught something interesting at the other end of the lunch table. Brady Brootski was stuffing a carrot stick into Ivana's milk carton when she wasn't looking.

Lizzie imagined she was a sports announcer,

telling what happened next, play-by-play. "Laaaadies and gentlemen! Ivana takes a drink. She gulps carrot instead of milk. She puuuulls it out of the milk carton with her teeth and spits it across the table at Brady. He ducks. It bounces off the lunchroom monitor's belly.

"What a move, laaaadies and gentlemen! The table goes wild! The monitor does not laugh. She points to the *Poor Manners* table and marches Ivana away. Brady laughs so hard, he chokes on one of his Twinkies. The score is tied."

. . .

The sound of the three o'clock bell was sweet to Lizzie. "Free," she whispered to herself. When she reached into her locker for her backpack, she saw a note sticking out of the front pocket. *If you read* The Celery Stalks at Midnight *tonight, you can get two points tomorrow. Your buddy, Ivana.*

When Lizzie unzipped her backpack, there lay the book. For the first time that day, she smiled. Maybe Ivana the Terrible wasn't so terrible after all.

Grandma Lil was right where she said she would be—parked under the spreading chestnut tree across the street. She honked and waved. It wasn't necessary. Lizzie could have spotted Grandma Lil in a crowd. She wore her clown suit with the dancing bears in pink tutus and her pink clown wig that looked like cotton candy. Her stage name was Pinky.

"Don't want my beauty to get hot," she said as Lizzie tossed her backpack into the front seat. The beauty was really a beast, a beat-up 1975 canary yellow Buick. Looks didn't matter to Grandma Lil. She saw beauty inside even beastly things. Lizzie disappeared in her grandmother's bear hug. Grandma Lil was an enthusiastic hugger.

"How was your first day?" she asked.

"I'd like to forget it," replied Lizzie.

"That bad, huh? Make any new friends?"

Lizzie didn't answer. Instead she looked out the window at the pairs of friends talking and laughing on their way to the buses. It made her feel lonely and small. She wished making a new friend were as easy as making cheese and crackers. Was there a recipe for making a friend?

"You will," Grandma Lil answered for Lizzie. "Just remember, to make a friend, you must be a friend. Now take a peek in the backseat. You'll find a friend there."

Lizzie craned around. "Samson and Delilah!" She squealed at the sight of her guinea pigs. They darted back and forth across their cardboard box. Lizzie gently scooped them up one at a time and buried her nose in their long golden hair.

"Thanks for bringing them along, Grandma. You're the best."

"You are, too, angel."

. . .

"Done!" said Lizzie five minutes before bedtime. She had just finished reading *The Celery Stalks at Midnight* when her grandmother came in to say good night. Lizzie looked forward to their bed-time chats. At home with her father, their house was quiet. Most of the time they ate supper with few words between them. Then her father liked to watch television. Lizzie spent a lot of time alone in her room, reading. Books let her travel to a million places.

They chatted a bit about their day, Grandma Lil more than Lizzie. Talking nonstop, she told about the puppet show she put on at the chil-dren's hospital. Lizzie liked to listen to her ram-ble on enthusiastically.

When Grandma Lil said, "Lights out," Lizzie threw her arms around her neck and they hugged for a long moment. Then Grandma Lil asked Lizzie the question she asked every night. "How will you remember this day?" Lizzie didn't hesi-tate to answer. "I'll remember it as the day Lizard met Ivana the Terrible." Then she closed her eyes on her grandmother's puzzled look and drifted off to sleep.

Chapter 3

March 31

Dear Ivana,

It was fun in the library this morning. Did you see the stuffed pink pig riding the Harley? It's one hundred points! That's what I want to get Grandma Lil. She would love it. She and my grandfather used to ride motorcycles all across the country. Then he died and she stopped riding. I don't know if she can fit on a motorcycle anymore. I just tested on *Tales of a Fourth Grade Nothing*. Now I'm up to twenty-five points! I have a long way to go. I just checked out *The Voyages of Doctor Doolittle*. It's for older kids. I could get twenty-six points. Do you think I can do it?

> Your buddy,
> Lizzie

Dear Lizzie,

My bullfrog, Buster, has the fastest tongue in the West. He can catch a fly quicker than I can snap my fingers. Why don't you come to my house and meet him? I have thirty-five points now. You're catching up fast. Between you and me, we'll put so many dots on the cheetah, he'll look like a black panther! I'm reading *The Curse of the Trouble Dolls*. It's a good book. I'd like to put a curse on Brady.

> Your buddy,
> Ivana

P.S. Will you sit with me at lunch?

The timer beeped and all the kids quickly
traded journals, eager to read what their buddy
had written. Lizzie wondered what Ivana was
like away from school, away from everyone pok-
ing fun at her. It might be fun to go to her house
and meet Buster. Lizzie had never met a pet bullfrog before.

When she read Ivana's P.S., Lizzie got nervous. It was easy to write to Ivana in the journal, but it was hard to talk to her. Ivana was bold. Nothing scared her. If kids made fun of her, she stuck up for herself. Lizzie couldn't even look her in the eye and say hello. Before she returned Ivana's journal, she wrote back: *P.S. Tiffy and Crystal asked me to sit with them first. Sorry.*

"Go to Ivana's stupid house?" Brady blurted out behind her. He'd been reading her journal over her shoulder. Lizzie felt like a mouse in the shadow of a hawk. She snapped the journal shut. Ivana heard him. Lizzie could swear her hair began to writhe. "Why, you . . ."

"Brady, Mrs. Flannigan is here." Lizzie sighed at the interruption. Mrs. Lula stepped into the hall to talk to Mrs. Flannigan for a minute.

Brady slammed his books together. He yanked Ivana's hair on his way out. She grabbed for his braid and missed, then shot out her leg to trip him. Brady was too fast for her and leaped over it like a jump rope. "See ya," he sneered, "wouldn't wanna be ya."

"At recess you're mine, Bratski," Ivana said.

Lizzie wondered who Mrs. Flannigan was and why Brady seemed so mad.

.   .   .

Tiffy and Crystal's chatter flew in Lizzie's ears as she struggled to unstick her tongue from the roof of her mouth.

"Why are you making those weird faces?" Tiffy asked Lizzie.

"Really," said Crystal. "It looks like you swallowed a moth."

Lizzie peeled off the top slice of her wheat bread. "My grandmother forgot the jelly," she said, staring down at her sandwich, thick with peanut butter.

"Oh," said Tiffy.

"Here," said Crystal, handing Lizzie her own carton of milk. "You need this more than I do."

"Really," said Tiffy. "Got milk?"

All three of them laughed.

"Who's Mrs. Flannigan?" asked Lizzie.

"She's the teacher for morons like Brady who can't read," Tiffy answered.

So that's why Brady whispers out loud and points at the words when he reads, thought Lizzie. She didn't like Brady. He was a big pest. Still, it bothered her when Tiffy made fun of him like that. She wanted to tell her so. But she didn't. She choked down her words along with the peanut butter.

Instead she told them about her Peruvian guinea pigs. "Their hair's golden and silky and as long as a pony's tail. I roll it up every night with tiny quilt scraps from my grandma Lil's rag basket. If I don't, they'll chew their hair off."

"I think their hair would be a lot more fun to comb than Barbie's hair," said Tiffy between bites on her celery stick.

"I do, too," Crystal agreed. "That would be a lot more fun."

At recess, the girls played freeze tag. "You're it," Tiffy cried, and tapped Lizzie's head. Tiffy and Crystal ran off, giggling. It didn't take long for Lizzie to tag and be tagged again. From where she stood frozen in a running position, she could see Ivana at the swings. Her eyes were closed, and she was smiling and swinging so high it seemed she would sail into the sky. Ivana couldn't see what was about to happen next, but Lizzie could. Brady Brootski was sneaking up behind her.

Lizzie unfroze her vocal cords long enough to shout across the playground, "Ivana, watch out!" Ivana turned in time to see Brady reach out and push her off course. The swing began to twist wildly, and Brady doubled up in laughter. In a daring leap Ivana propelled herself out of the swing and landed amazingly on both feet, as surefooted as a cat. Then she took off after Brady.

Lizzie was so mad, she wanted to take off after him, too. But she didn't. She stood frozen in position, a perfect statue, until the bell rang.

Chapter 4

April 8

Dear Ivana,

   My grandma said I could come to
your house on Saturday. I can't wait to
meet your water-walking lizard you
wrote about yesterday. Can he really
run across the top of the water? It
sounds impossible.

                    Your buddy,
                    Lizzie

After Ivana read Lizzie's journal entry, all she
wrote back was, *Cool beans!* Then she drew her a
map to her house. It looked like this:

Saturday came fast, too fast. Lizzie was a little nervous about going to Ivana's house. She didn't know what to expect. Ivana's house stood apart from the other houses. They were small, wood frame, and looked mostly alike. Ivana's house was a big red barn. Grandma Lil just said, "Not something you see in the city limits every day."

Lizzie caught a glimpse of Ivana in the back-yard, flapping around in a blue, oversized Dallas Cowboys football jersey. She plucked a running pass out of the air.

"Touchdown!" Ivana cried out. A boy tackled her. "No fair," she yelled, spitting grass out of her mouth. "Time-out."

"Bye, Grandma," Lizzie said softly.

"I'll be back in two hours. Will that be enough time?"

Lizzie nodded. *Maybe too much time,* she thought.

"Call me on my cell phone if you need me."

Just as Grandma Lil pulled away, Ivana came running up to Lizzie, out of breath. "Hey, come play with us." She doubled over to catch her breath. "I'm playing football with my brothers. The only rule is"—she huffed and puffed—"no blood, no foul." Lizzie had never touched a football, much less played the game.

The backyard sort of looked like it did in Ivana's drawing. There was a beat-up bread delivery truck parked at the end of the lot. This was Ivana's old school. She wrote to Lizzie that her mom had home-schooled her until she had to go back to work. There was Ivana's "sunflower forest" and fort and apple tree.

"Heads up!" her brothers called, and Lizzie looked up just in time to see a football spiraling at her face. She caught it out of pure luck. "Awesome catch," they said, and circled around to congratulate her.

Ivana had written about her brothers in her journal, so Lizzie quickly figured out who was who. There was Surge, the biggest and brawniest. Then came Mouse, so named because his pointed nose made him look like one. The youngest was Pony. He got his nickname from the ponytail he'd worn since he was four. Now he was twelve.

"Can't you say hello to Lizzie first before you start throwing stuff at her?" Ivana asked.

"Hello, Lizzie," they said. She smiled and blushed.

"Hey," said Surge, "you can be on Ivana's team. She needs all the help she can get."

"No, I don't. I can take you on any day," she boasted.

"Oh, really. Take this," Surge said. He tucked her under his arm as easily as if she were a football and ran across the yard with her. Ivana kicked and screamed the whole time. "Touchdown," he cried, and let her drop to the ground. Lizzie laughed. Ivana acted mad, but Lizzie could tell she really wasn't. She pulled a handful of grass and threw it at her brother's head while he did a victory dance.

"Wash up, kids. Soup's on," Ivana's father called from the back porch. Ivana introduced Lizzie to her father. Now Lizzie knew where Ivana got her black hair from. Ivana's father took off his oven mitt to shake her hand. "I'm glad you're here," he said. "You're the first school friend Ivana has invited to the house."

There was that word again, *friend.* Lizzie wasn't

sure why Ivana even liked her. Lizzie remembered what Grandma Lil had said: "To make a friend, you need to be a friend." Lizzie didn't feel like she had been a friend to Ivana. She didn't sit with her at lunch or play with her at recess. Lizzie was afraid if she played with her at school, the other kids would make fun of her as much as they did Ivana. Still, she didn't make fun of Ivana the way the other kids did. She felt like her friend when they wrote to each other in their journals. And she was beginning to feel like her friend now.

"I wish you could meet Ivana's mom, but she's selling her baskets at a crafts fair today," Ivana's dad said. "Maybe next time. I hope you like black bean tacos."

When Lizzie stepped into the house, she expected to see cows and sheep running through it. Instead it was fixed up like a normal house, sort of. It had high ceilings and rafters and a spiral staircase leading to the upstairs. Art was everywhere. Children's drawings were mixed in with framed art. One whole wall in the kitchen looked like it had been finger-painted. The house was a dance of color, like a flower bouquet.

Lizzie nibbled at her taco. There was so much talking, laughing, and joking going on at the table, she felt like a character in a play. A character without a speaking part.

"Hey, Lizzie," Ivana said. "Show them the penguins."

Lizzie liked to keep the penguin picture on her desk at school to remind her of her dad. Her father had mailed the picture to her after his ship left the Antarctic.

Lizzie pulled the picture out of her plastic "flower power" purse and shared it with everyone.

"Cool beans!" said Mouse.

"Lemme see," said Pony.

"What is it?" asked Surge.

"You tell him, Lizzie," said Ivana.

"When my dad's ship stopped at the Antarctic, he played a game of football with the other sailors on the ice. And, well, they had fans."

They all laughed at the comical penguins flocked on the sidelines, watching the sailors play football. Lizzie laughed, too. It felt good to be a part of a family, even if it was someone else's.

After lunch Ivana showed Lizzie the "zoo" in her upstairs bedroom. Lizzie preferred cuddly animals but was amazed at Ivana's collection of amphibians and reptiles. Ivana warned her not to touch her eyes after she held Fig, her fire newt.

His protective slime coat might make them sting. They shared a tense moment when Neptune, the green anole lizard, leaped out of Lizzie's hands and hid in the forest of junk under Ivana's bed. They finally found him perched on top of her Super Soaker gun.

Ivana let Lizzie walk Iggy the iguana on a leash up and down the stairs and showed her a giant pickle jar, home to the two salamanders Ivana had caught at a creek. Lizzie didn't pet Grump, the snapping turtle. He wasn't in a good mood. The water-walking lizard really did run across the top of the water in his aquarium, like a magic track star.

"This one's still my favorite," Ivana said, lifting Buster out of his red bucket. She set her very fat, brown bullfrog on the floor. The girls lay on their bellies, facing him, watching his eyes stare, then blink, and his throat throb.

"I think he knows how to do a smart pet trick," said Ivana. "Watch this." She whistled through her fingers, and Buster hopped to her.

"Wow," said Lizzie. *Buster had to be the coolest pet*, she thought. *Well, second coolest after Samson and Delilah.*

"When I grow up," Ivana said, "I want to be a jungle biologist. I want to study wildlife all over the world. What do you want to be when you grow up?" she asked Lizzie.

Lizzie hesitated to answer. She had never told anyone before. It was her secret. But Ivana had shared her dream, and Lizzie wanted to trust her.

"It's dumb," said Lizzie. "Promise not to tell."

"Promise," said Ivana.

"A forest ranger," Lizzie muttered.

. . .

At bedtime Grandma Lil couldn't squeeze in a word anywhere. For once Lizzie did all the talking.

She talked so much and so fast about her day, she sounded like an auctioneer at a sale. Her grandmother turned out the lights and asked Lizzie her favorite question. "How will you remember this day?"

Lizzie's smile faded a bit, and a touch of melancholy settled in her eyes. "As the day I wished I was raised in a barn with lots of brothers."

Chapter 5

April 24

Dear Ivana,

I'm nervous about family show-and-
tell tomorrow. I'm going to bring my
penguin picture. I got a letter and a
new picture from my dad I'm going to
show, too. He's in Greenland now. I
have a picture of him feeding a silver
fish to a harbor seal. He's smiling at me.
My dad, I mean. Not the seal. What will
you bring for show-and-tell?

Your buddy,

Lizzie

P.S. Do you want to come to my house tonight and do homework? I have something neat to show you.

April 24

Dear Lizzie,

    I'm excited about show-and-tell. Mine is going to be a big surprise. I can do something nobody in class can do (I bet). Guess what? I tested on the book you showed me in the library—*Ferret in the Bedroom, Lizards in the Fridge.* I got eight points. I have almost one hundred points now!

Your buddy,
Ivana

P.S. Did you finish reading *Doctor Doolittle*?

    Ivana's journal made Lizzie nervous all over again. Last night she and Grandma Lil had finally finished *Doctor Doolittle* and did a little jig around the bedroom when they read the words *The End*. It had taken her more than three weeks, with her grandmother's help, to read the entire book. Lizzie thought of all the things that would have been easier to do than that—climbing a mountain; walking on water like the water-walking lizard; getting Brady to stop bugging her and braiding her hair during silent reading time.

She wrote a P.S. back to Ivana. *Yes, I did finish* Doctor Doolittle. *I'm scared about the test. The only thing I remember is that he could talk to animals.*

Ivana's P.S. simply said, *Yes*. And then, *Do you want me to bring Buster?*

. . .

"Cool beans! What is it?" Ivana asked, her face Christmas morning happy.

Lizzie walked through her bedroom door, holding a giant stuffed animal in front of her. She and Ivana had just finished their math homework and were practicing their family show-and-tell presentations. It was fun doing homework with Ivana. She figured things out for herself and didn't ask to copy Lizzie's paper like Tiffy and Crystal did all the time. Lizzie let the creature flop down on her bed beside Buster.

"It's a wallaby. Wilma Wallaby," said Lizzie. "Ask me what's in it."

"Okay," said Ivana, playing along. "What's in it?"

"Go fish," said Lizzie, pointing to the pouch.

Ivana set down the apples she held, quickly slipped her hand in, and just as quickly jerked it back out. "ARRRGHHH!" she growled like a caveman.

"It's alive," said Lizzie in a spooky ghost voice.

"Hey! I thought you said this thing was stuffed," complained Ivana.

"It is stuffed—with something," said Lizzie. "Go ahead. Try again. Gently. They won't bite."

"What won't bite?"

"You'll see."

Ivana snaked her hand back into the pouch. Lizzie watched the pouch bulge and squirm as Ivana's hand made its way to the bottom. When she emerged with her catch, Lizzie clapped, causing the wriggling, golden guinea pig baby to squeal. Ivana buried her nose in its fur. "Hey, Lizzie, why didn't you tell me?" she demanded.

For two weeks now Lizzie had burned with the

secret. But she wanted to wait and surprise Ivana once the babies were old enough to handle.

"There's two more," said Lizzie.

Ivana reached in and pulled out the second little pig, also golden. When Ivana fished out the final, snowy white pig, she gasped, "It's beautiful."

Lizzie asked Ivana which she liked best.

"Eeny, meeny, miny, mo. Catch a guinea by his toe. If he squeals, call him bro. Eeny, meeny, miny, mo. This one," said Ivana, scooping up the white one.

"Call him bro?" asked Lizzie, puzzled.

"Remember my bro, Mouse? Whenever he catches me wearing his Emmit Smith football jersey, he squeals like Whitey here."

The girls shared a laugh and then choked on their own giggles when they set the babies loose on the bed. Buster hopped toward them, spooking them into a wild scurry under the pillow.

"Enough fun," said Lizzie, gently returning the babies to their mother.

"Poor Samson," said Ivana, lifting him out of his box in the corner. She Eskimo-kissed him. "Why is Daddy all by himself?" she cooed at Samson.

"Because the last time Delilah had a baby, Samson killed it," Lizzie explained. "I didn't get it out of the cage quickly enough. This time I did."

Before she returned Samson to his shavings, he tinkled on her. "Oooo. I've been slimed!" squealed Ivana.

"Wheep, wheep, wheep!" squealed Samson in response.

"Now you know how I feel sitting in front of Brady Bratski," said Lizzie. "I get slimed every day."

A great shadow fell across the girls. Casting it was Grandma Lil, standing in the doorway,

dressed in her dancing pink bears clown suit, all set to show parents how to make balloon animals at Parents' Night. "You girls ready or not?" she asked.

"Ready," said Lizzie.

"Not," said Ivana, lifting out the snowy white baby for one last snuggle.

Chapter 6

April 25

Dear Ivana,

   If I choke today during show-and-tell, please help me. Guess what? I forgot to tell you. I made thirty points for *Dr. Doolittle!* Now I have sixty-five points. I need thirty-five more to get the Harley pig. I don't really like reading for points. I would rather read for fun.

                          Your buddy,
                          Lizzie

P.S. Brady won't stop braiding my hair. It

drives me nuts. I'm going to start
wearing a bun.

April 25

Dear Lizzie,

   If we don't do show-and-tell
immediately, I'm going to eat my apples.
I'm starving. I woke up too late for
powdered doughnuts. My brothers ate
them all. I had to eat soggy cornflakes.
I hope the day gets better. I'm in a bad
mood. Will you sit with me at lunch
today?

Your buddy,
Ivana

P.S. You're like me. I read books for the
fun of it, too!

    Lizzie had made up her mind. She was going to
sit with Ivana at lunch today. Who cared what the
other kids thought? Since she had started school
at Morningside a month ago, Ivana had asked her
almost every day. Lizzie kept making excuses.

One time she had asked Tiffy and Crystal if Ivana could sit with all of them. They teased her for it the rest of lunch and recess, too. "She is such a Froot Loop," said Tiffy. "I *eat* Froot Loops. I don't eat *lunch* with them."

Tiffy volunteered first to show-and-tell. "My pom-poms once belonged to my grandmother. They're an heirloom." She bounced into a cheer that began: "*S-U-C-E-S-S*. That's the way we spell success!"

Erma Malone raised her hand. "Excuse me, Mrs. Lula, but don't you spell *success* with two *c's—s-u-c-c-e-s-s?*"

"Why, yes, you do," replied Mrs. Lula. Erma scribbled down the word on the personal spelling list she always kept on her desk.

"*S-u-c-c* . . . whatever . . . who cares?" Tiffy exclaimed. She finished by saying, "And now I would like to let my friend Lizzie hold one of my pom-poms for the *rest* of the day."

Several girls broke into sighs and whispers. Lizzie blushed red. She hid the pom-pom in her lap.

"That was very good, Tiffy," said Mrs. Lula. "Since you volunteered first, you may pick who goes next."

"I pick Lizzie."

Lizzie gulped. She had hoped to be last. She wanted the time to run out. As she stood up, the pom-pom fell out of her lap. *Oh, great,* thought Lizzie, *way to be a geek.* She put the pom-pom in the chair and picked up her pictures.

Slowly she moved to the front, where she faced twenty pairs of blinking, staring eyes. They looked like curious forest creatures. Creatures with sharp teeth. She quivered and took a deep breath to begin.

"Are you okay?" asked Mrs. Lula.

"She's okay," blurted out Ivana. "Go ahead, Lizzie. Tell them about your dad and how he and the sailors played football with the penguins and how he sent you a picture of a harbor seal from Greenland. Go ahead and tell them."

By the time Ivana finished, Lizzie had very little left to tell. *What a relief,* she thought. Lizzie cleared her throat and in a quavery voice finished telling about her dad's adventures at sea. She held the picture up in front of her face as she talked.

"That was nice, Lizzie. Now you pick who goes next," said Mrs. Lula.

Several kids signaled to her hopefully. Lizzie looked over at Ivana. She was polishing an apple at her desk. "I pick Ivana."

Ivana stomped to the front, then turned to face the audience. "I brought apples," she began. "My gramps lives in the Appalachian Mountains. He grows an apple orchard there. I visit him every summer. He lets me eat all the apples I want. One time I ate an apple with a worm in it. It was really sweet and juicy. The apple, I mean. When I saw that worm all bit in two and squirming around, I felt terrible."

Mrs. Lula's face turned pea green.

"Last summer my gramps taught me something else you can do with apples besides eat them." Lizzie knew what was about to happen. One by one Ivana tossed the three apples into the air and began to juggle them. For once, nobody made a crack or snickered. Everyone stared, openmouthed. *How wonderful,* thought Lizzie. She felt like she was at the circus. At the finish Ivana tossed an apple to Lizzie, another to Mrs.

Lula, and bit into the third. The entire class clapped, Lizzie most of all.

Lizzie proudly set her apple on the corner of her desk. It was so shiny, she could see her reflection in it.

"Better not eat it, Lizard—it's probably poison," Brady whispered to the back of her head.

Lizzie turned around and shot back, *"Be quiet!"*

Their eyes locked in a stare down. Her glasses reflected in the pupils of his eyes. Brady winked. "Make me, Lizard."

Lizzie ignored him and tried to listen to the rest of show-and-tell. But she couldn't see. Ivana's hair blocked her view. Her hair, wild as snakes, seemed alive. Lizzie stared at it. She could swear it moved sometimes. She wanted to touch it. She had to touch it.

Very gently Lizzie poked her pencil through a curl and twirled it around the tip, fascinated, when WHOMP! Brady Brootski shoved his desk into hers and Lizzie's desk slammed into Ivana's like a train wreck. Lizzie, without knowing what was happening, poked her pencil point into the back of Ivana's head, and her apple went flying off her desk.

"Ouch! That hurt!" Ivana cried, rubbing the back of her head. Horrified, Lizzie quickly cast down her eyes.

"Mrs. Lula," Brady called out. "Lizzie stabbed

Ivana in the back of her head." He howled like a hyena.

"SSSSHUT up, you walking, talking wart mouth," hissed Ivana. "Lizzie, why did you poke me?" Ivana asked.

"Stop being mean to Lizzie," Tiffy scolded Ivana. "She doesn't even like you or your stupid apple. See," she said, picking up the apple off the floor, "she threw it away."

For once Ivana didn't stick up for herself. She slumped down in her chair while Mrs. Lula checked the back of her head for damage. The teacher sent Lizzie and Ivana both to the time-out booths for disturbing the class. As Lizzie was marched to her punishment, she already knew how she would answer her grandmother's question that night. She would remember this day as the day she made her first enemy.

April 30

DEAR IVANA,

YOU'VE BEEN MAD AT ME FOR FIVE DAYS.
WHY WON'T YOU READ MY JOURNAL? CAN YOU
SEE THESE BIG LETTERS? I DIDN'T POKE YOU ON
PURPOSE. IT WAS BRADY'S FAULT. I DIDN'T
THROW THE APPLE. IT ROLLED OFF MY DESK. I
EVEN WASHED IT OFF AND ATE IT AT LUNCH.
WILL WE EVER BE FRIENDS AGAIN? IF YOU
READ THIS, YOU WILL KNOW THE TRUTH.

STILL YOUR BUDDY,

LIZZIE

P.S. I almost have enough points to buy

the Harley-Davidson pig for my grandma.

P.P.S. Delilah's babies are growing fast.
But I guess you don't care.

April 30

Dear Lizzie,
    Blah, blah, blah, blah. Yak, yak, yak,
yak. Yuk, yuk, yuk.

Not your buddy,
Ivana

P.S. Watch out. I'm going to beat
everybody at Supersonic Reader.

. . .

"Where do you want to eat tonight?" asked
Grandma Lil. "Frank's Furters?"

"I'm tired of Frank's Furters," said Lizzie. And
she was. Plus hot dogs made her miss her father
even more. It made her remember all those times
they spent hunkered over a campfire, roasting
wieners. She and her grandmother ate out almost
every night. Grandma Lil hated to cook but kept
saying she needed to get back in the habit with
Lizzie there.

"How about here?" Grandma Lil said, and pulled into a parking spot underneath a giant ice-cream cone blinking in the sky. They had just come from Parents' Night at Children's World Learning Center. Grandma Lil had put on a puppet show and was still wearing her Pinky costume. It used to embarrass Lizzie going out in public with her grandmother dressed like that, but it didn't bother her anymore.

After they ate their hamburgers, they picked out their favorite flavor of ice cream and sat outside on a white bench. Together they took their share of rest and happiness, eating peppermint ice cream under a rising moon. Grandma Lil slipped out of her clown shoes and tapped her bare toes on the cement. Lizzie did the same.

Grandma Lil talked on and on about Parents' Night but finally noticed Lizzie wasn't saying a word. "You're really quiet tonight, angel. Is something wrong?"

Everything was wrong. Where should she start?

"I still don't have a best friend at school," she said. "Tiffy and Crystal like me more than I like them. They make fun of people too much. And they're bossy."

"What about Ivana? I thought you liked her,"
said Grandma Lil.

"I did, kind of. I do. But she doesn't like *me*
anymore."

"How do you know?"

Lizzie told her grandmother all about their mis-
understanding. "She scoots her desk as far away
from me as she can. Like I have chicken pox or

something. It really irritates me when she does that."

Grandma Lil pulled Lizzie close. In that embrace she felt warm and safe and loved. "Real friends find ways to make up again."

．．．

At bedtime Grandma Lil asked Lizzie to reach under the pillow.

Lizzie fished around and pulled out a sparkling golden necklace. A pearl as bright as the moon was set in the middle of a golden heart. "I wore this when I was a girl. My best friend gave it to me after we had a fight and made up."

"It's beautiful, Grandma," she said as her grandmother fastened the necklace around Lizzie's neck.

"Hard to believe something as beautiful as a pearl comes out of something as ugly as an oyster," Grandma Lil said.

"Really," added Lizzie.

"Do you know how an oyster makes a pearl?" Grandma Lil asked.

Lizzie shook her head.

"If something gets inside the oyster's shell and

irritates it, like a grain of sand or a small worm . . ."

"Sand and worms. Yuck. If I swallowed something that gross, I'd spit it out," exclaimed Lizzie.

"So would I," her grandma agreed, chuckling. "But the oyster doesn't. It squirts out a special substance that surrounds the irritant. It builds layers of circles until a pearl forms."

Lizzie looked down at her pearl and smiled.

After Grandma Lil left her room, Lizzie couldn't sleep. She tossed and turned and socked her pillow, trying to get comfortable. Soon she heard her grandmother's snores drifting down the hall. Lizzie slipped out of bed and sneaked all three baby guinea pigs into the bed with her.

She snuggled them and talked to them. "Do you like my necklace?" she asked. "It's easier having a pet for a friend than a girl," she told them. "You never get mad at me or make fun of me."

She petted Samson in his separate box. "I know you miss your family," she said, and thought of her father away at sea. She wondered if her dad

missed her as much as she missed him. She plumped the miniature pillows she'd put in the aquarium for the three babies and put them back in. Happy to be back home, they made soft grunts as they nursed from their mother.

In a week or two they would be ready to leave Delilah. Lizzie wondered if they would forget her like she had forgotten her own mother. Lizzie was so young when she died; she wished she could remember her. She often wondered what it would be like to have a mom to snuggle up with, like the baby guinea pigs did with their own mother now.

She lay in bed for a few moments and studied the pearl. The reflection of the moonlight made little rainbows bounce off it. Lizzie felt like she held a precious piece of sky in her hand. She imagined she was an oyster forming a pearl inside her. "If something gets stuck in your heart and bothers you," she whispered to her pets in the dark, "turn it into a pearl."

Chapter 8

May 5

Dear Ivana,

Delilah's babies are so cute. I like their ears most of all. They are big and funny looking. Delilah is a good mother. She cuddles them all the time. Guess what? I have seventy-five points now. I just need twenty-five more to get the Harley-Davidson pig! I hope nobody else gets him first.

Your buddy,
Lizzie

Dear Lizzie,

Mrs. Lula checked our journals. She said I had to write normal stuff to you. We get our STAR test scores today. Big deal. When we took the test, Mrs. Lula said if everybody passes, we get a pizza party. Whoop-de-do. You weren't here for the test, but I bet you can still have pizza.

Ivana

"Class," Mrs. Lula called. "Now for the big moment. I'm going to pass out the STAR test scores. These are confidential, so keep your score to yourself."

"Do we get a pizza party?" asked Tiffy as Mrs. Lula passed out their tests.

"No. Not everyone passed. But I'm still proud of all of you. I think you tried your hardest, and that's what counts. Now let's break into reading groups."

On their way to groups, students let each other peek at their test scores. Brady Brootski made an airplane out of his. He flew it into Ivana's head. It caught in her hair. She pulled it out and unfolded it.

"Hey, don't look at that," Brady said, trying to grab it back from Ivana. He wasn't fast enough. Tiffy snatched the test out of Ivana's hand. "I want to know who made the class lose the pizza party," she said. Before she could unfold Brady's test, however, Ivana snatched it back.

"It's none of your business," she said, then she crumpled the paper into a ball and threw it at Brady.

"What's wrong with you, Ivana? Were you raised in a barn?" snapped Crystal, wrapping her bubble gum around her tongue.

Lizzie felt her neck grow hot. She was tired of everyone picking on each other, especially on Ivana. For the first time she dared to speak up.

"Yes! She *was* raised in a barn!"

Brady started mooing like a cow.

Goofed again, thought Lizzie when she saw Ivana's lips pucker up like she'd just sucked a bitter lemon. "I didn't mean it . . ." Lizzie didn't have the chance to add "as an insult," because Ivana spat hateful words at her.

"And you, Lizzie Gardener . . . you—you want to be a forest ranger when you grow up!" Ivana stammered.

Fire rushed to Lizzie's cheeks as everyone started laughing at her.

"A forest ranger? Who's your superhero? Smokey the Bear?" After Brady finished howling at his own joke, he turned on Tiffy. "Look here, nosy," he said to Tiffy, uncrumpling the paper. They all leaned in to peer at his score. Lizzie couldn't believe her eyes. Brady had passed.

"Humph," huffed Tiffy. "*Pure* luck," she said, and stuck her nose in the air.

"I showed you mine. Now you show me yours," he challenged her.

"We'll show *you*," said Crystal, her voice as snippy as scissors.

She held up her score. It was only ten points higher than Brady's. "Show him, Tiffy. Just show him who's smarter," said Crystal.

Tiffy hid her test behind her back. Her bottom

lip began to quiver. "It's nobody's business," she announced, ripping her test in two as she flounced back to her desk.

. . .

At lunch Lizzie ate alone. Tiffy and Crystal sailed past her with their trays. They had ignored her all morning after she confronted them. Lizzie looked down at their end of the table. Crystal shot her a dirty look and started whispering to Tiffy. Lizzie's tuna fish sandwich smelled too horrible to eat. She missed her dad's cooking. Lizzie snapped her carrot stick in two and bit down hard. *Way to go,* she thought. *I already lost one friend. Now I've lost two more.*

"Ouch, you hit a tangle," Lizzie complained to Grandma Lil later that night.

"Sorry. I'm trying to make you feel better—not worse. You know when I had a really bad day at school, my mom would curl my hair in rags. We didn't have curling irons and hot rollers in those days. The next morning, my curls came tumbling down. It made me feel like a princess in a fairy tale."

"I'll never feel like a princess. I'm under a curse," Lizzie replied.

"Let's give it a try," said Grandma Lil.

Maybe with curls, people would notice her more and even like her, at least a little, Lizzie hoped.

Chapter 9

May 12

Dear Ivana,

I don't care if you beat me at Supersonic Reader. So you can stop bragging. I read all the time because I like to. Not for stupid points. I don't care if nobody likes me. Who would? I mess up all the time. I wish Mrs. Lula was here today. It's going to be a bad day.

I give up,

Lizzie

P.S. Remind me not to ever tell you a secret again!

Lizzie spent the rest of journal time drawing black swirlies in her notebook. As the swirlies grew into tornado size, Lizzie's thoughts twisted around, too. *Why won't she believe I was just sticking up for her? I can't believe my hair looks like this. I wish I'd never let Grandma Lil curl it with those rags. Now I look like a clown—not a princess. Listen to me, Ivana. I wouldn't ever make fun of you.*

When she felt Brady's hand reach for her hair, she jerked it from his grasp. "Keep your paws to yourself. I'm having a bad hair day."

The timer beeped, and the girls traded journals.

May 12

Dear Lizzie,

I'm sorry I told your secret. I was wrong. My mom said you were just sticking up for me. Now Brady makes barn animal noises at me all the time. Can I still come to your house and see the baby guinea pigs?

Will you be my buddy again?

Ivana

P.S. I brought someone with me you might like to see.

P.P.S. What did you do to your hair?

First thing that morning their substitute had stood before them with fists planted on her hips and a scowl on her face. "Mrs. Lula is sick today. I will be your teacher. I am Huffensnort. *Mrs.* Huffensnort."

After journal writing, she turned her back to the class to write directions on the board. Brady leaned forward in his desk. He aimed his words at Ivana. "Wonder what made Mrs. Lula sick. Did ya give the old witch one of your poisoned apples?" he asked, and grunted like a pig.

Lizzie watched Ivana's hair begin to twist and writhe. She knew what was coming. She slid *way* down in her seat. Ivana slowly turned. She shot her gaze over the top of Lizzie's very curly head and fired at Brady, "Mrs. Lula's not an old witch, TOAD boy."

Mrs. Huffensnort called out, "No talking."

She marched them through their math lesson. Then she said, "Your teacher wants us to do art today. So we will do art. For homework you were supposed to bring something you would like to draw and tell about. Any volunteers?" she barked. No one dared raise a hand. Except Ivana.

"You, young lady. What did you bring?"

Ivana lifted the lid off her shoe box and whistled. Out jumped Buster. Ivana set him on a lily pad she found in the pond near their school. He sat there like a frog with very good manners. "Buster's my best friend. I found him near our goldfish pond when I was chasing my ball one day. Kinda like the princess who finds the talking frog when she drops her golden ball down the well. She kisses him and breaks the evil spell and he turns back into a handsome prince. I've never kissed Buster, though."

"Ribbit," said Buster. Everyone laughed.

"I know what'll happen if you kiss him," Brady called out. "He'll croak over dead. Get it, croak?" He let his head thunk down on his desk like he was dead.

Everyone laughed at Ivana except Lizzie.

"That's enough!" declared Mrs. Huffensnort. "As for you, mister." She pointed at Brady. "You'll stay in from recess! Now," she huffed, "let's do *art!*"

During art, Brady drew a picture of Ivana turning into a frog and taped it onto the back of her red Texas Rangers baseball jersey. Her shirt was so baggy, she didn't feel it. Lizzie pulled the picture off and gave Brady a dirty look.

When Mrs. Huffensnort announced five minutes to clean up, art supplies disappeared into drawers and cabinets. Lizzie watched Ivana gently set Buster down in the shoe box and replace the lid.

"Everybody but Mr. Brootski is dismissed for recess," Mrs. Huffensnort said.

Ivana tucked her shoe box under her arm and headed for the door.

"Young lady, where do you think you're taking that frog?"

"To recess," Ivana answered.

"No animals on the playground. Leave him here with me. I will watch him."

Ivana frowned but returned Buster to her desk. She whispered through the airholes poked in the lid on Buster's box: "I'll be back soon. Don't be lonely."

Lizzie knew how Buster felt. After everyone left, she asked Mrs. Huffensnort in a very small voice, so Brady couldn't hear, "May I have the potty pass?"

Once in the bathroom stall, Lizzie sat down and started pulling at her hair. She wanted to tame her curls. "This will take forever," she complained aloud. Now she bent down her head and started shaking it vigorously like a wet puppy. She hoped the curls would get so tired, they'd go limp. She heard the door beside her squeak

open and slam shut so hard, it shook her stall walls like an earthquake. Even her toilet seat rumbled.

Curious now about her neighbor, she leaned her head down far enough to peep under the stall wall. A very large pair of black rubber-soled shoes, rolled-down hose, and hairy legs greeted her view. Lizzie popped back up on her seat, her eyes wide as her dad's Sunday morning pancakes. That's no third grader, she realized immediately. That's Mrs. Huffensnort.

. . .

After recess Ivana flopped into her seat and took the lid off the shoe box. Lizzie could hear the rustle of grass. "Where are you?" Ivana cried into the box. She looked under her desk. Then it happened again. Ivana's hair began to writhe. Lizzie caught her breath as Ivana leaped onto Lizzie's desk and held the empty shoe box high above her head. "Who stole my frog?" she shouted across the room.

When she turned the shoe box upside down, grass fell on Lizzie's head. Her curls, as grasping as octopus arms, held the blades in place.

"I want him back. No one leaves here until I get Buster back!"

Lizzie looked around the room. The entire class sat still as stone. Even Mrs. Huffensnort stood fixed in her place. No one moved. No one breathed. But the spell lasted only a moment. Brady Brootski broke it with his hyena laugh.

Mrs. Huffensnort bellowed at Ivana, "Go to the principal. NOW!"

Ivana stormed out, slamming the door behind her. Mrs. Huffensnort scribbled a discipline note and told Lizzie to deliver it to the principal. Lizzie didn't want to, but she had never told an adult no in all her life. She didn't know how. Obediently she rose from her desk.

"Go for it, Smokey Bear," Brady mouthed under his breath.

In that very second, Lizzie felt something new spring up inside her. Brady's comment set it off. How could she protect wildlife one day? She didn't even know how to protect a friend.

She was going to start now. But something stopped her. Something sticking out of Brady's *Planet Blasters* comic book. Something that was going to get Brady Brootski into a mess of trouble. Instead of griping at him, she turned her back on Brady. She smiled sweetly at the substitute, said, "Yes, ma'am," and left the room.

She expected to see Ivana in the principal's office. Instead Lizzie almost tripped over her in the hall. Ivana was slumped on the floor, her head buried in her arms. She was crying.

Lizzie crumpled the discipline note and let it fall to the floor. She flopped down beside Ivana and finally worked up enough courage to tap her on the shoulder.

Ivana looked her right in the eye, and for the first time Lizzie didn't look away. She didn't turn to stone, either. Ivana's eyes weren't mean or scary enough to turn anything to stone. No. Her eyes were very beautiful. As dark and bright as black diamonds glistening in the bottom of a deep, clear pond. Lizzie took Ivana's hand. "Come on," she said. "We're going to rescue Buster."

Ivana looked puzzled, then wiped her sleeve across her face. She let Lizzie lead her.

Lizzie "Lizard, Smokey the Bear" Gardener and

Ivana "the Terrible" Romanov marched back into the classroom and directly to Brady Brootski's desk.

"Mrs. Huffensnort, Brady Brootski stole Ivana's frog," Lizzie declared. "I can prove it." Lizzie snatched a lily pad from the pages of Brady's *Planet Blasters* comic book. The same lily pad belonging to Buster the bullfrog.

Mrs. Huffensnort's fists flew to her hips. "MR. BROOTSKI!" she boomed. "Return that frog. NOW!"

"Yeah, where's Buster? We want Buster," the class chimed in.

"So search me," Brady said, pretending innocence. "I don't have her bullfrog. Besides, Mrs. Huffensnort was here."

"I know Mrs. Huffensnort went to the bathroom. Sorry, Mrs. Huffensnort," Lizzie quickly added, then proceeded. "You were alone in the room during recess, Brady. You're the only one who could have taken him," Lizzie insisted.

Lizzie wouldn't give up. She kept hammering Brady with accusations until finally a loud RIB-BIT erupted from Mrs. Huffensnort's lunch sack.

The substitute opened it, and out hopped Buster.

Ivana swooped him up and kissed him on his slimy brown frog lips. A hush fell across the room. Would the frog become a prince? Lizzie wondered. No, he wouldn't. But she thought something just as wonderful happened. Mrs. Huffensnort didn't send Ivana to the office after all. She banished Brady Brootski instead.

Chapter 10

May 13

Dear Ivana,

Grandma Lil used horse mane shampoo, conditioner, and a comb with big teeth to get all the grass and curls out of my hair. Boy, was Mrs. Lula mad. Did you see her turn colors when she read Mrs. Huffensnort's note? Who are you going to apologize to? I guess I should say I'm sorry to Mrs. Huffensnort since I told the whole class she went to the bathroom.

Your buddy,
Lizzie

May 13

Dear Lizzie,
   I won't apologize to anybody.
Everyone should apologize to me. Even
Mrs. Huffensnort. She said she'd watch
Buster and she didn't. But I guess I'll
make up something. I don't want to miss
recess for a week.
                    Your buddy,
                    Ivana

P.S. Thanks for sticking up for me.

When Mrs. Lula had returned the next morning and read the note Mrs. Huffensnort left, she turned as pea green as the day Ivana told her she'd eaten half a worm. "No fun, all work!" she announced. Lizzie had never seen her so steamed. For punishment she gave extra homework. "Everyone in this class owes an apology of some sort. Decide who deserves your apology, and create that apology for homework tonight. Anybody who comes tomorrow without an apology will lose recess privileges for a week!"

Lizzie figured she owed Mrs. Huffensnort an apology for telling on her for leaving Brady alone in the classroom. So that night she drew a picture of a potty pass and wrote on it: *I am sorry for telling a tattle, Mrs. Huffensnort. Your friend, Lizzie Gardener.* Then she colored in hearts and flowers and angel cats all over the rest of the potty pass.

When Lizzie eased into her chair the next morning, she sat on something hard. She reached under her and pulled out a present that looked like a gorilla had wrapped it. The yellow ribbon curled as much as her hair had yesterday.

Lizzie pulled off the lid, and there, on top of torn-up comic pages, lay a beautiful red hair bow. A hastily scribbled note read: *I'm sorry. From your secret admirer.* Beside the signature was a picture of a cheetah like the one on the back wall. The only person who owed her an apology was Brady Brootski, and he wasn't the kind of boy who gave girls a red hair bow.

"Now, boys and girls, it's time to turn in your apologies, either to me or each other," said Mrs. Lula, her arms crossed.

"Psst, Lizard," said Brady. "Pass this to Ivana. Don't you dare look at it, either," he added. Lizzie took the envelope from his hand and tapped Ivana on the back with it. Ivana turned around, licking shut an envelope. "Here, Lizzie, I figure I need to apologize to you." She and Lizzie exchanged envelopes.

Eagerly Lizzie read Ivana's note: *Dear Lizzie, Sorry I dumped grass on your head. You were having a really bad hair day, and I made it worse.* Now Lizzie knew who had given her the red bow. She smiled and tucked the note back in the envelope.

Curiosity teased her enough to take Brady's dare. Peering over Ivana's shoulder, she discovered a wonderful drawing of Buster, wearing a golden crown. On the bottom, in the worst cursive Lizzie had ever seen, a note read: *Sorry for being mean to you and Buster. Thanks for telling Tiffy off when she tried to snag my STAR test.*

Ivana stomped back to his desk. Her hands flew to her hips. "Brady!" She called out his name like a drill sergeant. "I accept your apology. But don't you ever pull a rotten trick like that again. Now shake my hand," she commanded, shoving her hand in his.

For the first time that year, Lizzie and Ivana sat down to lunch together. They chatted and traded food like they had been friends forever. When the lunch monitor turned her back, Ivana showed Lizzie a surefire way to catch M&M's with her mouth every time.

Just before the bell rang, Lizzie thanked Ivana for the hair bow.

"What bow?" asked Ivana.

"The one you left on my chair this morning. This one," said Lizzie, fishing it out of her backpack.

"It wasn't me," she said.

Lizzie, confused, showed Ivana the note. It happened again. Ivana's hair began to twist and writhe, but her head popped back up with a smile. "Nice cheetah," she said. "I know who gave you the red hair bow."

"Who, who?" Lizzie hooted like an owl.

"The same person who drew the cheetah in our classroom."

"Who, who?"

"The same person who drew that great picture of Buster this morning."

Now it was Lizzie who turned pea green.

Chapter 11

May 18

Dear Ivana,

   I am really sad today. The Harley-
Davidson pig is gone. I looked in the
library window this morning, and he's
missing. Someone else got him before
I could. I only needed five more points.
I'll never find another one like it. I
guess I'll buy my grandma the butterfly
bracelet. But I really wanted the pig.

                    Your buddy,
                    Lizzie

Dear Lizzie,

I have turned into a book maniac. My brothers call me Bookworm Woman. I'm going to read a book every day this week. The awards assembly is Monday. I want to win. I want to be the top, number-one Supersonic Reader. I want to write a book called *After Supersonic Reader, the World!* Don't be mad if I beat you. Let's race.

Your buddy,
Bookworm Woman

Lizzie was pretty sure she had more points than Ivana. At the last cheetah spotting, they had been close. Still, she hadn't started a book all week, she was so upset about the Harley-Davidson pig. She didn't want to race. Ivana kept slipping books into Lizzie's backpack, but it did no good. By Thursday, she still had only ninety-five points, same as Monday. That night Grandma Lil coaxed her into finishing *My Friend*

Flicka. That had taken her almost as long to read as *Doctor Doolittle.* The next morning at library time, she tested on the computer, passed, and earned twenty points. But Lizzie didn't seem to care anymore. She turned in her book and left without checking out another one.

. . .

As soon as the farmer led the speckled hog on-stage the following Monday, the awards assembly

went wild. Clapping, whistling, cheering, stomping, and the sounds of squeaking balloon hats bounced off the walls. Room mothers had made the hats for everyone to wear after Grandma Lil showed them how at Parents' Night.

It's a wonder, thought Lizzie, *the poor hog doesn't run away out of pure fright.* But he didn't. He just sat there. Blinking, looking bored, like he was thinking, I'd rather be taking a mud bath. He acted as if this was any other ordinary hog thing to do . . . grunt, eat corn, wallow in the mud, kiss a principal . . . big deal.

Lizzie wished she could sit on the stage with the hog and be as far away from Brady Brootski as she could get. He sat behind her and Ivana. He had just blown a whistle in her ear and numbed it. Ivana numbed her ears even more. She turned around and hollered, "Stop blowing that whistle in my ear or you'll be wearing it in yours!"

Brady stopped blowing the whistle, but as soon as Ivana turned around, he aimed a pointy pencil at her balloon hat. Lizzie snatched it away from him just in time.

When Mrs. Hog turned on the microphone, it

made such a sharp ringing sound that everyone covered their ears and groaned. The hog started squealing. It took the farmer several minutes to calm him down. "I hope he's potty trained," Lizzie whispered to Ivana, and they both laughed.

"Good morning, boys and girls. Welcome to the third-grade awards assembly. I am proud to be handing out several awards today for outstanding achievement." Mrs. Hog began calling out the winners. They came up onstage, shook her hand, and got their certificate. Lizzie clapped so much before they got to Mrs. Lula's class, her hands were beet red by then. She decided to give them a rest for a while.

"And now, boys and girls, I want to announce the prize you've all been waiting for. Who will be principal for the day? Altogether, the entire third grade made three thousand fifty-three Supersonic Reader points!" Everyone cheered. "The class who made the most was Mrs. Lula's. They had a thousand five."

Mrs. Lula's students went goofy, making faces at each other, laughing, saying "YES," and squeaking each other's balloon hats.

"Also from Mrs. Lula's class comes our top Supersonic Reader."

Everyone looked around at Mrs. Lula's kids, wondering who it would be. Lizzie was sure it was Ivana. All week long she'd had her nose in one book after another. Lizzie had barely been ahead of her when she stopped reading.

"This Supersonic Reader had a total of one hundred fifteen points. Lizzie Gardener, come on down!" Lizzie was shocked to hear her name called. She turned to Ivana, who smiled and said, "I didn't take the tests. I wanted you to win. If I were principal, I'd send everyone to the office." She gently pushed Lizzie out into the aisle.

The applause that washed over Lizzie made her feel shy and ten feet tall all at once. Mrs. Lula gave her a standing ovation. Onstage Mrs. Hog shook her hand like she was a water pump and handed her a really neat certificate with a golden seal. It had her name and award in fancy cursive letters, *Lizzie Gardener, #1 Supersonic Reader,* and listed her points. Mrs. Hog asked her to remain onstage, then called up the rest of Mrs. Lula's class.

"Now, girls and boys," she addressed them. "I would not do what I am about to do for just anyone. But I will do it for you. Why? Because Mrs. Hog promised to if any one class managed to make one thousand points. And Mrs. Hog always keeps her promise."

With that, their principal bent down and gently planted a big wet one right on his kisser. Wild delight rocked the room. Balloon hats popped. Camera bulbs flashed. Cheers and whistles ricocheted off walls. And in the middle of it all stood Lizzie Gardener, her principal, her classmates, and one happy hog, wearing very bright, very orange lipstick.

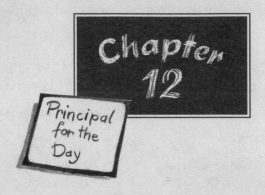

Chapter
12

Principal
for the
Day

May 29

Dear Lizzie,

We just get to be best buddies, and
you have to leave. No fair. It's no fun
without you here. We're going to have
show-and-tell today. The theme is
friendship. I brought something for you.
Now you're gone. I miss you.

Your buddy,

Ivana

It was the day school let out for summer vacation. For show-and-tell Mrs. Lula had asked

everyone to draw names and bring a gift for that classmate. Who you drew was supposed to remain a surprise, but everyone was swapping names and whispering what their surprise was to everyone else. Everyone except Ivana. She sat at her desk, wearing a big frown, pulling at the blue curly ribbon on her gift and watching it boing back in place.

Tiffy volunteered first. "The friend I will never forget from my third-grade year . . ." She looked around at everyone to make them think it was them. She smiled really big at Ivana, then turned her head in the opposite direction and said, ". . . is Crystal."

A knock on the door interrupted them. "Class, we have a special guest today."

Everyone turned to the door. Mrs. Lula opened it and in stepped their guest, dressed in a dark blue business suit, a starched white shirt with a dog-eared collar, a pearl necklace, and a name tag that read *Principal for the Day.*

"Principal Gardener brought a gift she would like to share," said Mrs. Lula.

Lizzie looked very official. She didn't feel nearly as shy as the last time she'd stood in front

of her class. And today nothing was falling down, not even her kneesocks. Grandma Lil let her wear nylons and bought her a brand-new pair of navy blue shoes. She felt very grown-up.

Lizzie and Mrs. Lula ducked behind the teacher's desk and surfaced with an aquarium. They set it on top of Mrs. Lula's desk. Lizzie invited her classmates up to see. "Today I brought my Peruvian guinea pigs, Samson and Delilah. I have to keep their hair curled up in little rags or they'll chew each other's hair off. It's a natural instinct."

The class replied with "oh, nos" and "oh, my goshes."

Some of the boys pretended to chew on the girls' hair.

"Make them go to the office," the girls appealed to Lizzie before everyone asked her all kinds of questions about the guinea pigs.

"Now, here's the best part. Delilah had three babies six weeks ago." Lizzie lifted out a golden one. "They love to eat Cream of Wheat. Come and pet them—with your petting finger," she added, wiggling her pinkie.

The kids circled around the aquarium, eager to get close to the babies. Everyone used their petting finger. The babies made soft, happy squeals in response.

"I'm going to give this baby to the friend from third grade I will never forget."

When Lizzie placed the snowy white guinea pig into Ivana's cupped hands, it snuggled right up to her. She flashed her toothy smile and held it close to her ear to hear the squeaky little sounds the guinea pig made. The baby began to wriggle. It got tangled in Ivana's wild nest of hair. "Wheep, wheep, wheep," it cried.

As Lizzie tried to free it, Ivana laughed. And for the first time ever, the class laughed *with* her. Not *at* her. Even Brady Brootski. Finally Lizzie untangled the baby and returned her to Ivana's waiting hands. "Now Buster will have a friend," someone in the circle said.

"That's right—you'll need a bigger shoe box for both of them," piped up another.

"Can a bullfrog and a guinea pig get along together?" asked Ivana.

"I don't know," said Lizzie. "I guess they could try."

The class laughed at the thought of a bullfrog and a guinea pig sharing a shoe box together.

.　.　.

That first night of summer vacation, Grandma Lil had a hard time finding a spot to sit for their bedtime chat. Wilma Wallaby, guinea pigs, popcorn balls, juice boxes, and Lizzie and Ivana, dressed in nightshirts and stretched out with coloring books and crayons, took up the entire bed.

"Close your eyes and reach under my pillow," said Lizzie.

"Did you lose a tooth?" her grandmother asked.

"No. You'll see."

Grandma Lil fished around under Lizzie's pillow. She pulled out something furry.

"Okay, open your eyes now," commanded Lizzie.

"Cool!" said her grandmother. "A pig on a Harley-Davidson."

"Ivana gave it to me at friendship show-and-tell. She bought it with her Supersonic Reader points and saved it for me so no one else would get it first. She knew I wanted it for you."

"Thank you, angel. Thank you, Ivana. What a sweet thing to do. And you know something? His smile reminds me of your grandfather's a bit." They all laughed.

"Grandma, can we stay up a little longer?" pleaded Lizzie.

"Okay, just a little, but I want to know one thing."

"Sure. I know. I know. How will I remember this day?" Lizzie answered.

"I don't know what Lizzie remembers," interrupted Ivana, "but I know how I'll remember it."

"How's that?" asked Grandma Lil.

"As the day Lizzie wore the red hair bow that"—Ivana stopped to mushy-kiss her pillow several times—"her *boyfriend* gave her!"

"You're terrible!" chuckled Lizzie. She hoisted her pillow and gave Ivana a solid *pow* on top of her head. War declared, the pillow fight was on.

"Cease-fire, cease-fire! I'm out of here!" yelled Grandma Lil, laughing and dashing for the door. She gently closed it on the sounds of thudding pillows, squealing pigs, and two giggling girls, fighting their way into friendship.

About the Author

C. Anne Scott is the author of the picture book *Old Jake's Skirts*. A teacher for more than ten years, Ms. Scott was able to draw on her recollections of favorite students when creating the characters of Lizzie and Ivana. Coincidentally, while writing this book, she and her son relocated to Alpine, Texas, where they both had to start at new schools, just like Lizzie.

About the Illustrator

Stephanie Roth has illustrated several books for young readers. As a child, Ms. Roth's family moved many times, so she knows firsthand what it's like to be the new kid in town. Ms. Roth lives in Burnsville, Minnesota.